WITHDRAWN

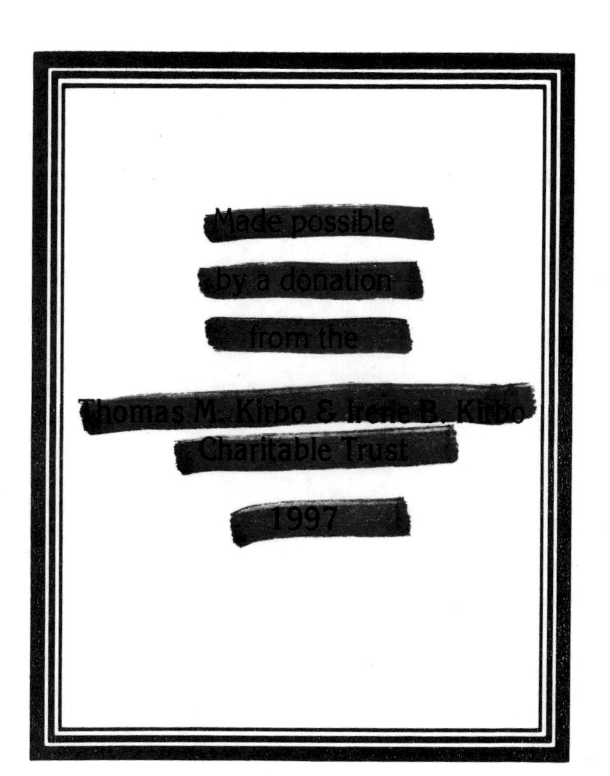
Made possible
by a donation
from the
Thomas M. Kirbo & Irene B. Kirbo
Charitable Trust
1997

MOSES

retold from the Bible and illustrated by

LEONARD EVERETT FISHER

Holiday House / New York

MOSES' LINEAGE

Abraham (+Sarah)

Isaac (+Rebecca)

Esau Jacob [Israel] (+Leah) (+Bilhah) (+Zilpah) (+Rachel)

Dan Naftali Gad Asher Joseph Benjamin

Reuben Simon Levi (+Otah) (+Milcah) Judah Issachar Zebulun

Gershon Jochebed Kohath (+ ?) Merari

Amram (+Jochebed) Izhar Hebron Uziel

Aaron Miriam Moses (+Zipporah)

Gershom Eliezer

And then came Samuel Benjamin, Gregory Byron, Jordan Lucas, Thomas Cuyler, Timothy Sebastian, Marion Corrina, Duncan Berry, Charlotte Chisolm, Harold James, Samuel Shepley and the rest unnamed, all lovingly descended from Meskin-Fisher, Cuyler-Perkins, and Halle-Briggs.

ACKNOWLEDGMENT
With thanks and appreciation to Marcia Posner and Rabbi Leonard Romm, for reading the manuscript and pointing the way with constructive advice as I wandered the desert with the Israelites of old.

Printed in the United States of America
First Edition

Library of Congress Cataloging-in-Publication Data
Fisher, Leonard Everett.
Moses : retold from the Bible and illustrated by Leonard Everett Fisher.
p. cm.
ISBN 0-8234-1149-4
1. Moses (Biblical leader)—Juvenile literature. 2. Bible. O.T. —Biography—Juvenile literature. 3. Bible stories, English—O.T. Exodus. [1. Moses (Biblical leader) 2. Bible stories—O.T.]
I. Title.
BS580.M6F554 1995 94-12131 CIP AC
222'.109505—dc20

THE EXODUS
c. 1220–1180 B.C.E.

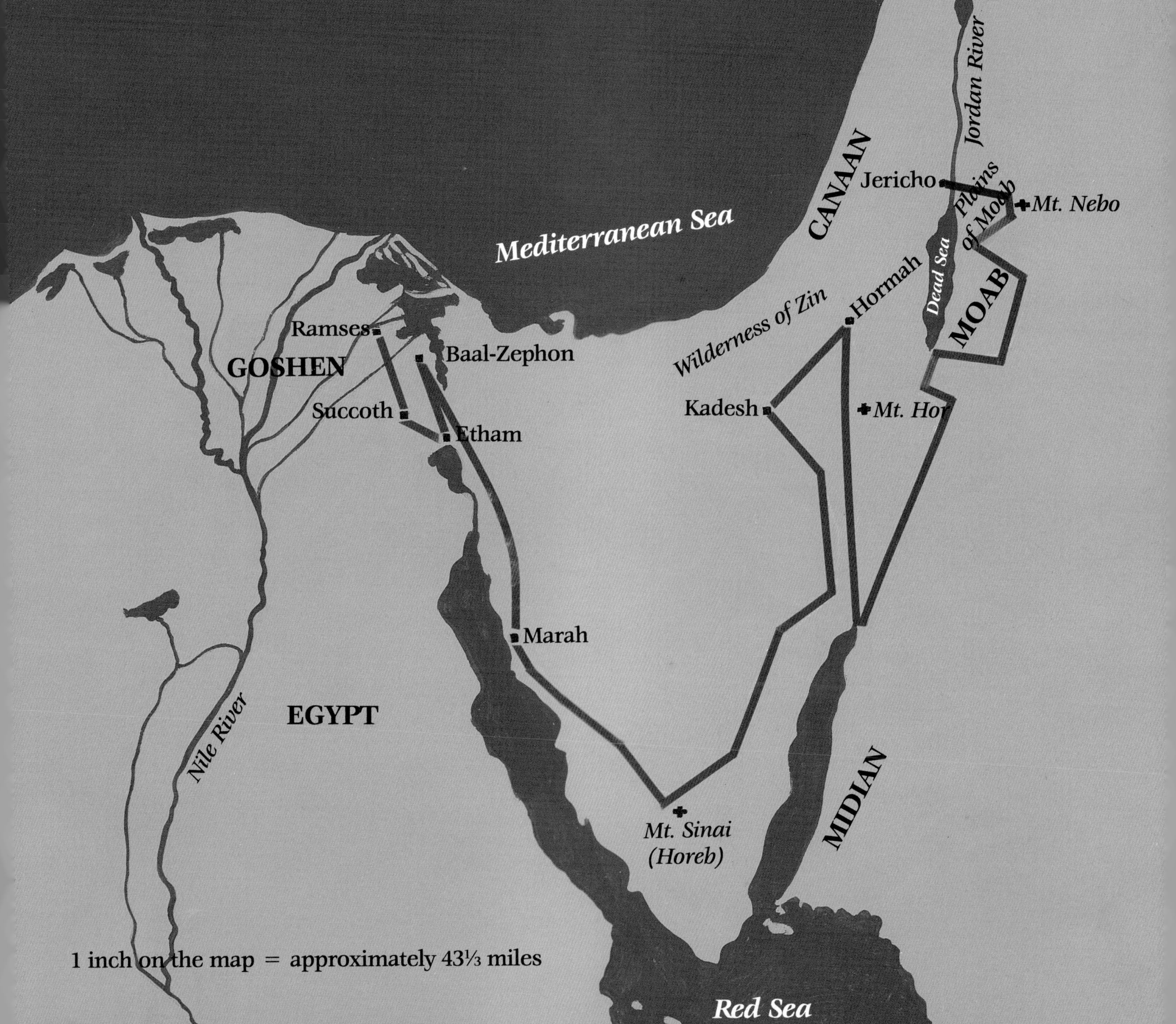

Billions of stars sparkled like diamonds in the Egyptian sky. A full moon lit the darkness like a giant lantern. The land and the river shimmered beneath. Nothing stirred but two dark shadows moving through the tall reeds along the riverbank.

"Here, Miriam, here is a good place," Jochebed whispered to her daughter as she gently placed a basket woven of bulrushes on the damp shore. Inside was Jochebed's infant son, Miriam's brother. "This baby must live. Look after him."

Jochebed crept away as silently as she had come, leaving Miriam hidden among the shadows of the river reeds, shivering with dread.

Three months earlier Pharaoh, the ruler of Egypt, had ordered that the newborn sons of his Israelite slaves be killed. "These Israelites do not worship our gods, only their own god. And their numbers keep growing. This is not good," he told his court. "One day they will take this land and this throne. We must kill their newborn sons. Now!"

From sunup to sundown, Egyptians had drowned nearly every newborn Israelite boy they could find. Now Miriam needed to protect her Israelite baby brother from being killed.

The long night ended as the sun climbed into the hot morning sky. The infant cried in hunger. Miriam watched as Pharaoh's daughter came to bathe in the river with her ladies-in-waiting.

"Listen!" the princess declared. "A baby cries! We must find it!"

Miriam went cold with panic as they found her brother. But the princess was gentle. She tried to soothe the hungry, bawling infant. "I shall call him *Moses,*" she said, "child of the river. I shall make him my son. But how shall I nurse him? He is an Israelite. It is forbidden for us to nurse Israelite babies."

Miriam stepped out of the reeds. "I can help you, Your Grace. I know an Israelite woman nearby who can nurse the child."

"Fetch her," the princess commanded. "The child is hungry!"

And so it came to pass that Miriam brought her mother, Jochebed, to nurse her own son and care for him in Pharaoh's palace.

Moses grew to manhood in the palace, not as an Israelite slave, but as the adopted grandson of Pharaoh himself. He learned to read, write, and behave as a prince of Egypt. Tall, handsome, kind, but with a quick temper, Moses was liked by both Egyptians and Israelites.

Even though Moses was raised as an Egyptian, Jochebed never let her son forget his people and his god. "You are an Israelite, the true son of Jochebed and Amram," she told him again and again. "You are the grandson of Kohath, great-grandson of Levi, and the great-great-grandson of Jacob called Israel, Patriarch of the Israelites."

One day, when Moses was forty years old, he came upon an Egyptian slavemaster beating an Israelite. "How dare you!" cried Moses and killed the slavemaster on the spot. When Pharaoh learned what Moses had done, he ordered him slain. Moses fled Egypt to the safety of nearby Midian just beyond Egypt's border east of Mount Sinai.

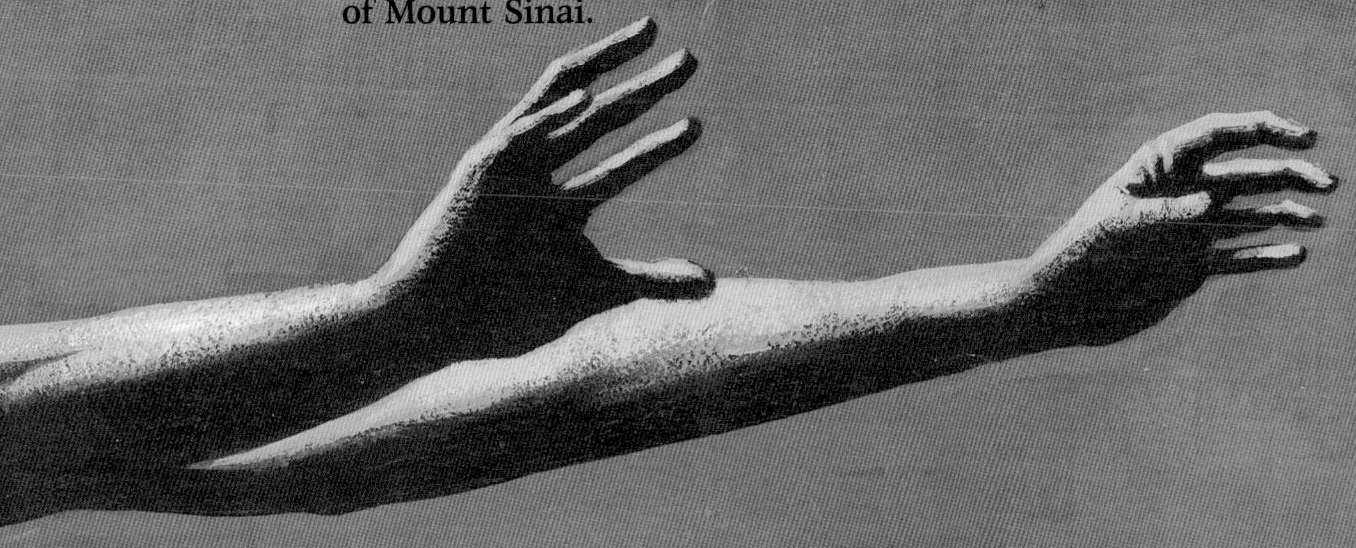

Moses came to a well where seven sisters were drawing water for their father's sheep. Some shepherds came and pushed the women aside, so they could draw the water first. Moses was so angry, he drove the shepherds off. When the sisters told their father, Jethro—also known as Reuel—that an Egyptian had come to their aid at the well, Jethro invited Moses to live with him and his family.

Not long after, Moses married Zipporah, one of Jethro's daughters. She bore him two sons, Gershom and Eliezer. And here Moses remained for forty years, in Jethro's house, tending Jethro's sheep.

When Moses was eighty years old, he spied a burning bush in a mountainous part of the desert. A booming voice spoke to him from the flames:

"Moses, Moses, Here am I. Put off thy shoes from off thy feet. Whereon thou standest is holy ground, I am the God of thy father, the God of Abraham, the God of Isaac, and the God of Jacob."

Filled with awe, Moses hid his face as God told him:

"I will send thee unto Pharaoh that thou mayest bring forth My people the children of Israel out of Egypt . . . unto a land flowing with milk and honey. And if the king of Egypt will not let you go, I will smite Egypt with all My wonders."

"Why have you picked me?" Moses asked. "I am too old. Who will believe me? Give me a sign that I might show the people." God showed His power. He turned Moses' wood staff into a snake and back again to wood. He told Moses that He could turn water into blood, too. "I do not speak well," Moses insisted. "I stutter and talk slowly. Who will listen to me?" God grew impatient with Moses' excuses. He told him that his older brother Aaron would join him and do the talking.

"Go!" God thundered.

And Moses went to Egypt with his wife and sons.

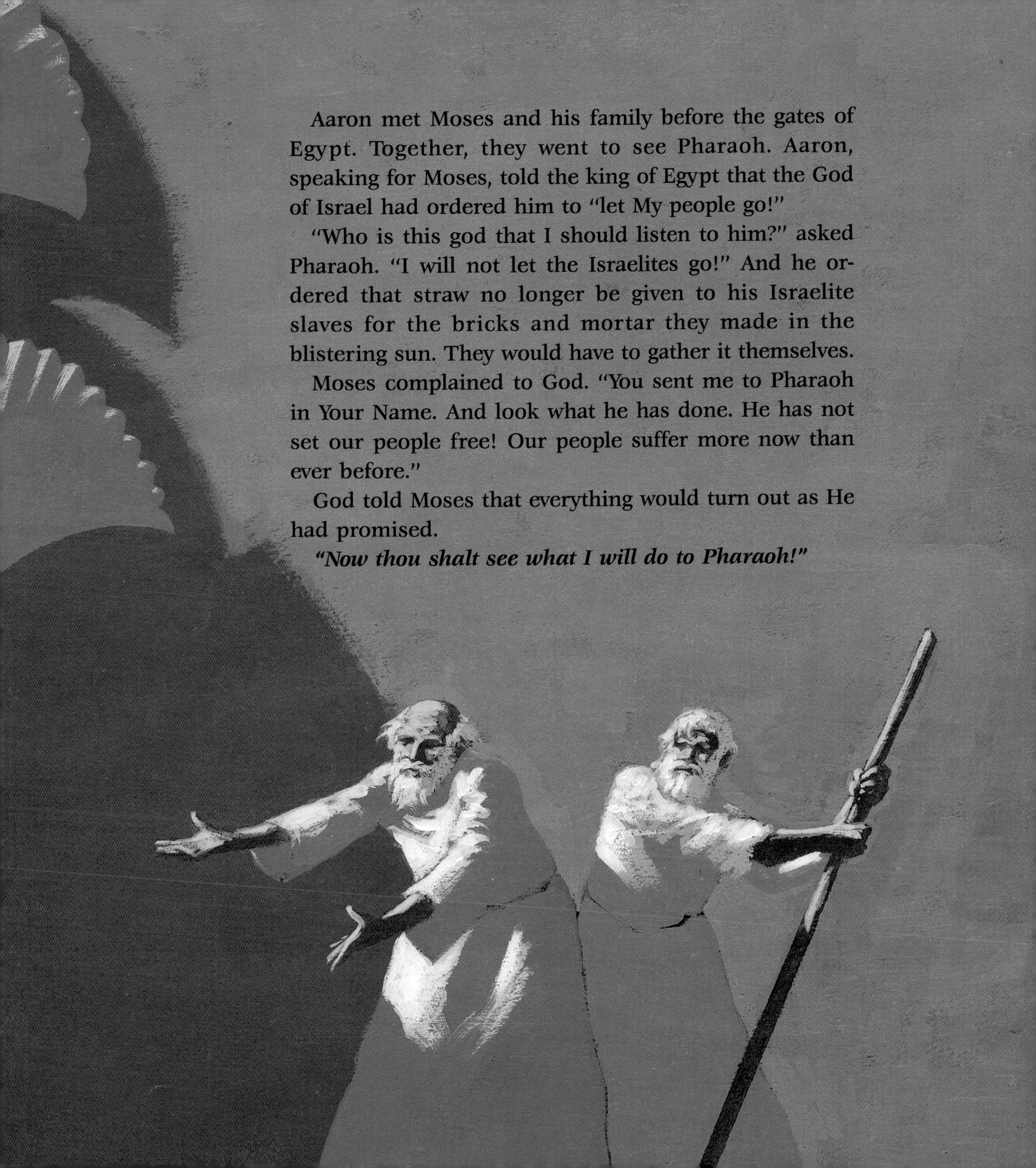

Aaron met Moses and his family before the gates of Egypt. Together, they went to see Pharaoh. Aaron, speaking for Moses, told the king of Egypt that the God of Israel had ordered him to "let My people go!"

"Who is this god that I should listen to him?" asked Pharaoh. "I will not let the Israelites go!" And he ordered that straw no longer be given to his Israelite slaves for the bricks and mortar they made in the blistering sun. They would have to gather it themselves.

Moses complained to God. "You sent me to Pharaoh in Your Name. And look what he has done. He has not set our people free! Our people suffer more now than ever before."

God told Moses that everything would turn out as He had promised.

"Now thou shalt see what I will do to Pharaoh!"

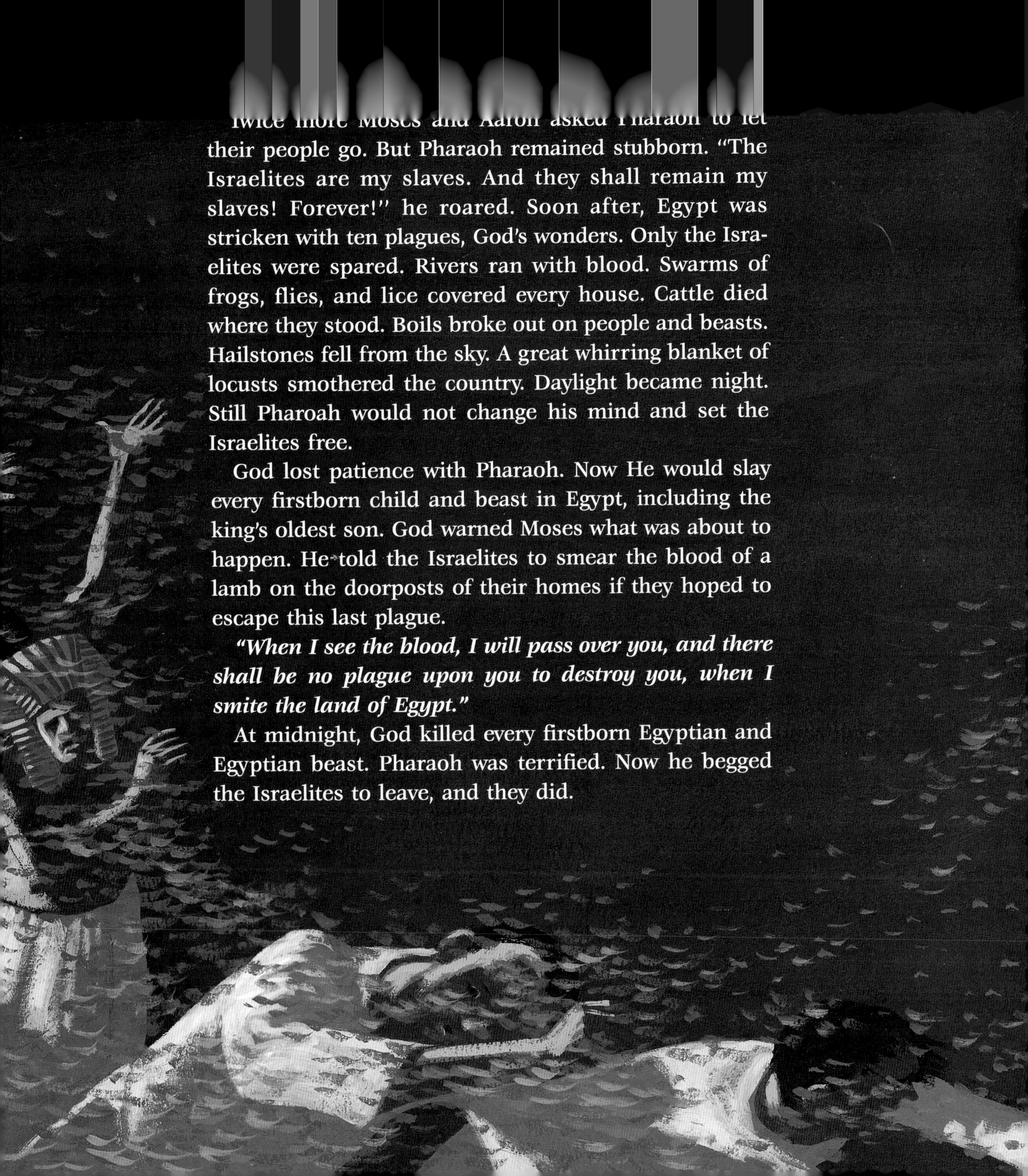

Twice more Moses and Aaron asked Pharaoh to let their people go. But Pharaoh remained stubborn. "The Israelites are my slaves. And they shall remain my slaves! Forever!" he roared. Soon after, Egypt was stricken with ten plagues, God's wonders. Only the Israelites were spared. Rivers ran with blood. Swarms of frogs, flies, and lice covered every house. Cattle died where they stood. Boils broke out on people and beasts. Hailstones fell from the sky. A great whirring blanket of locusts smothered the country. Daylight became night. Still Pharoah would not change his mind and set the Israelites free.

God lost patience with Pharaoh. Now He would slay every firstborn child and beast in Egypt, including the king's oldest son. God warned Moses what was about to happen. He told the Israelites to smear the blood of a lamb on the doorposts of their homes if they hoped to escape this last plague.

"When I see the blood, I will pass over you, and there shall be no plague upon you to destroy you, when I smite the land of Egypt."

At midnight, God killed every firstborn Egyptian and Egyptian beast. Pharaoh was terrified. Now he begged the Israelites to leave, and they did.

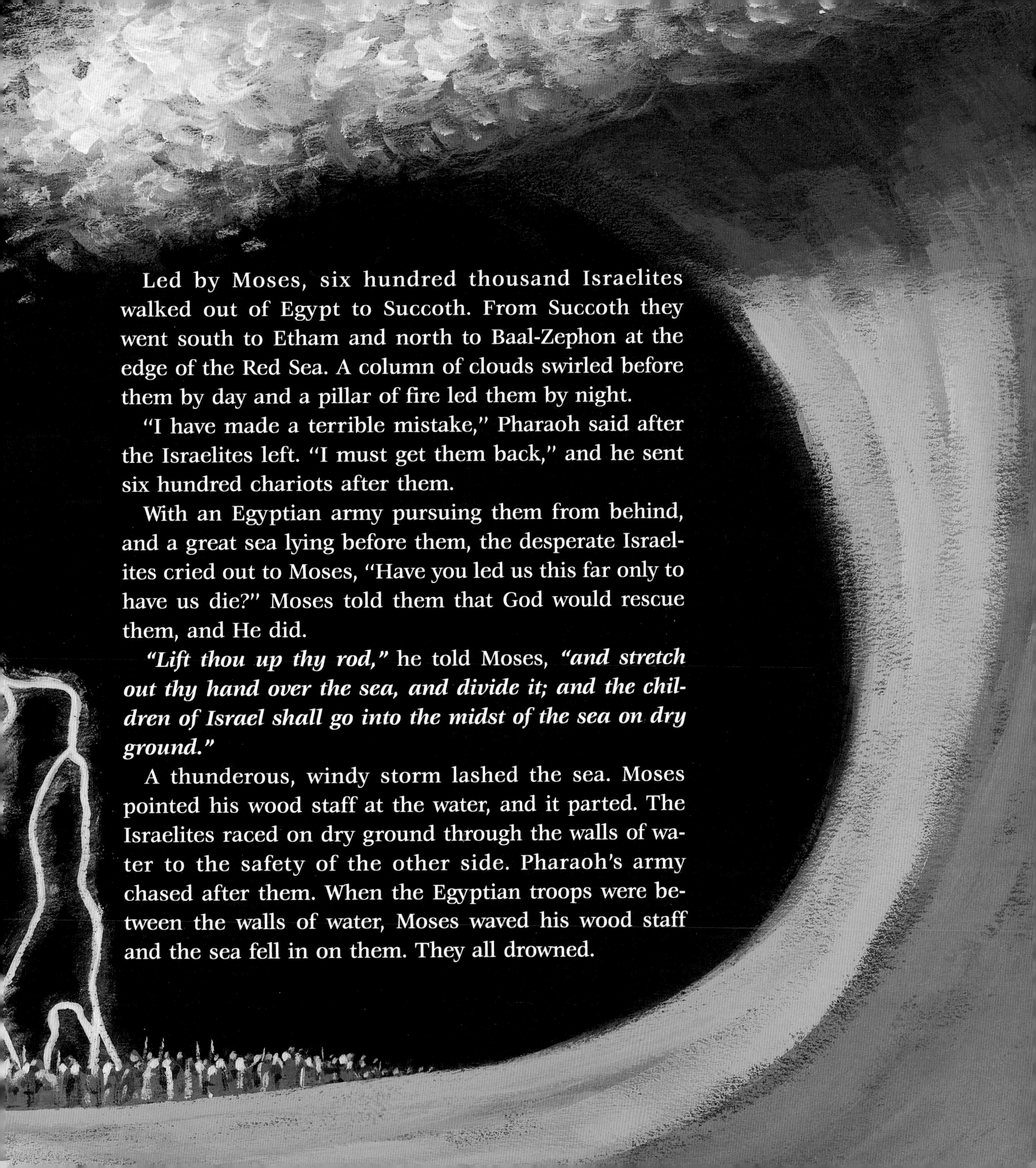

Led by Moses, six hundred thousand Israelites walked out of Egypt to Succoth. From Succoth they went south to Etham and north to Baal-Zephon at the edge of the Red Sea. A column of clouds swirled before them by day and a pillar of fire led them by night.

"I have made a terrible mistake," Pharaoh said after the Israelites left. "I must get them back," and he sent six hundred chariots after them.

With an Egyptian army pursuing them from behind, and a great sea lying before them, the desperate Israelites cried out to Moses, "Have you led us this far only to have us die?" Moses told them that God would rescue them, and He did.

"Lift thou up thy rod," he told Moses, *"and stretch out thy hand over the sea, and divide it; and the children of Israel shall go into the midst of the sea on dry ground."*

A thunderous, windy storm lashed the sea. Moses pointed his wood staff at the water, and it parted. The Israelites raced on dry ground through the walls of water to the safety of the other side. Pharaoh's army chased after them. When the Egyptian troops were between the walls of water, Moses waved his wood staff and the sea fell in on them. They all drowned.

Free at last, the weary Israelites continued on. There was neither water nor food in the desert, and the Israelites grew thirsty and hungry. Soon they came to Marah. But the water there was undrinkable.

"What shall we drink?" the Israelites asked. Moses sought God's help. God had Moses throw a tree into the water and the water became sweet.

Later, the people complained to Moses again. "You have brought us into this wilderness to kill us with hunger." Once more Moses asked God for help. That evening, as the sun set, the hungry Israelites found quail for their dinners. The next morning they found manna—a breadlike grain—to eat for their breakfasts.

The Israelites continued to complain. "You have brought us into this wilderness to kill us with thirst."

"What should I do with these people?" Moses asked God.

"I will stand before thee on the rock in Horeb; and thou shall smite the rock, and there shall come water out of it."

Moses did as he was told. He struck the rock. Water poured from it, and the people had water to drink.

In the third month after the Israelites left Egypt, they camped at the foot of Mount Sinai. It was hidden by a thick, thundering cloud that crackled with lightning. The ground moved and shook. Fires broke out near the mountaintop. God summoned Moses to the mountain and issued rules on how the Israelites were to conduct themselves to prepare for the giving of the Law. Moses took these rules to the people.

Three days later, the blast of a ram's horn roared out of the thundering cloud and crackling lightning. The Israelites trembled with fear. God had summoned Moses to the mountain where he disappeared for forty days and forty nights. Now God gave instructions on how to erect a holy meeting tent, the Tabernacle, and how to build a special chest, the Ark of the Covenant, to hold the Law which He was about to give. He told Moses that Aaron was to be the High Priest in the Tabernacle. And then He gave Moses the Law, including His Ten Commandments, which Moses was to reveal:

"Thou shalt have no other gods before Me. Thou shalt not make graven images. Thou shalt not take the name of the Lord thy God in vain. Remember the sabbath day, to keep it holy. Honor thy father and thy mother. Thou shalt not murder. Thou shalt not commit adultery. Thou shalt not steal. Thou shalt not bear false witness against thy neighbor. Thou shalt not covet thy neighbor's house, wife, servant, or anything that is thy neighbor's."

When God was through speaking, He gave Moses two stone tablets on which He had written the Law. But before Moses came down from the mountain, the Israelites had grown restless. Moses had been gone for forty days and forty nights. "We know not what has become of him," some Israelites said to Aaron. "Make us a god who shall go before us." And Aaron made them a god—a golden calf—out of their gold ornaments. Here was a dazzling creature they could worship with song and dance.

God was outraged. ***"Thou shalt have no other gods before me. Remember?"*** When Moses came down from the mountain, he saw the merrymaking around the golden calf. He, too, became outraged. He smashed the stone tablets, burnt the golden calf in a fire, and ground it to dust. Then he went back up the mountain to ask God to forgive them all.

God answered by having the three thousand Israelites who worshiped the golden calf slain. Then God sent Moses down the mountain again with a new set of stone tablets. He told him to lead his people on to Canaan, the land of milk and honey.

The people built a holy meeting tent, where they renewed their faith in God.

Moses led the Israelites to Kadesh, a city in Canaan. He sent twelve spies into the city to see how strong the people were. Forty days later they reported on what a rich place it was. Some of the spies described the high walls that surrounded the city and the fierce giants that lived inside. The Israelites were frightened. "Why did God bring us to this land knowing we might have to fight these giants?" they asked Moses. "We would sooner return to Egypt as slaves than be slaughtered in Canaan."

God was losing patience with the Israelites. Not only did they mistrust Him, but they lacked faith as well. ***"How long will they not believe in Me?"*** He asked. Again, Moses pleaded with God to forgive them. But God was too disappointed by the Israelites' refusal to enter Kadesh not to punish them. He sent a plague to destroy those spies whose reports had prevented the Israelites from entering the city. And He condemned the Israelites to wander forty years in the bleak desert until the older generation died.

"Your little ones, them will I bring in, and they shall know the land which you have rejected. As for you," God told the Israelites who displeased Him, ***"your carcasses shall fall in this wilderness."***

The Israelites followed Moses to the waterless Wilderness of Zin, north of Kadesh. The sun beat down on them like a flame. The Israelites complained about being in such an "evil place." Once again the people were thirsty. God told Moses to speak to a rocky cliff and water would come out.

Moses doubted that water could be had from the dry, stony wall of a cliff. He shouted to the Israelites, "Here now, you rebels, are we to bring forth water out of this cliff?" Whereupon, instead of speaking to the rocky cliff as God had commanded, Moses rapped it twice with his staff. Water poured out. God did not think that Moses should have shown such little faith.

He said to both Moses and Aaron: ***"Because ye believed not in Me, therefore ye shall not bring this assembly into the land which I have given them."***

Moses and Aaron could never set foot in the Promised Land.

The years went by and the Israelites stayed in the wilderness. The Promised Land seemed no closer.

Moses continued to act as God's voice to the restless Israelites. He wrote five books: *Genesis,* in which he told of the Israelite beginnings; *Exodus,* the story of their departure from Egypt; *Leviticus,* which contains all of God's laws, rules, and regulations; *Numbers,* the book that keeps track of the population while describing their trek in the desert; *Deuteronomy,* a farewell and summary of the first four. Moses was nearing the end of his life. Aaron had already died on Mount Hor in the Land of the Edomites at the age of 123.

Moses hoped that God would still let him enter Canaan.

"You shall drive out the inhabitants of the land," God had told him once, ***"and dwell therein; for unto you have I given the land to possess it."***

It was not to be. But God did show Moses the distant fertile land He had promised, from the top of Mount Nebo above the Plains of Moab. And there Moses died. He was 120 years old. He was buried in the Valley of Moab.

By the time the Israelites reached the Jordan River across from the city of Jericho, most of the older people that had come out of Egypt forty years before had died. A newer generation had nearly taken over. Joshua, a disciple whom Moses had chosen as his successor, led the Israelites across the river into the Promised Land. He conquered the Canaanites at Jericho, and ended forty years of Israelite wandering.

BIBLIOGRAPHY

——*The Holy Bible,* King James Version. New York: American Bible Society.

Dimont, Max I. *Jews, God and History.* New York: Simon & Schuster, 1962.

Durant, Will. *Our Oriental Heritage.* New York: Simon & Schuster, 1954.

Hertz, J. H., ed. *The Pentateuch and Haftorahs.* London: Soncino Press, 1966.

Jones, Alexander, ed. *The Jerusalem Bible.* New York: Doubleday, 1968.

Kastein, Josef. *History and Destiny of the Jews.* New York: Viking, 1933.

Toynbee, Arnold. *The Crucible of Christianity.* Cleveland: World Publishing, 1969.

MAPS

——*Atlas of the Bible Lands.* Maplewood, New Jersey: Hammond Inc., 1959.

——*Bible Lands and the Cradle of Western Civilization.* Washington, D.C.: National Geographic, 1946.